C Donelle Gress

·The Gourd Book·

WORDS MATTER

PUBLISHING

OUR WORDS CHANGE THE WORLD

Words Matter Publishing
P.O. Box 1190
Decatur, Il 62525
www.wordsmatterpublishing.com

ISBN 13: 978-1-953912-64-0

Library of Congress Catalog Card Number: 2022937084

Dedication:

The Gourd Book is dedicated to my loving, wonderful, passionate, and creative father who impacted my life in so many ways. It's a thank you for instilling the idea of following your dreams, living life with passion, humor, and love and for providing harvest of little signs from above to lead me to my destination.

Acknowledgements:

I'd like to thank my mom, my children and my significant other for their continued support and understanding of my undertakings. I'd like to thank Tammy Koelling for coming into my life and seeing the value and purpose of my work and helping bring it to fruition.

There was a man I loved so dear,
his name was Mr. Cleiman,
who spent every day and every night
daydreamin' and designin'.

One day he got the notion
to plant some seeds he found,
so he picked a spot, tilled up the earth
and tucked them safely in the ground.

And as the sun shined down on them
and the rain began to fall,
the little seedlings grew and grew
and became big and strong and tall.

Each day he passed the garden,
sometimes every hour,
wishing and hoping
the plants would bear a flower.

The fruit he found on the plants one day,
came in many shapes and sizes,
they grew so big and beautiful
he could not believe his eyes!

WOW!!

He bought himself a gardening book
to find out what he had grown,
because they were so unusual
and were from the seeds he'd sown.

He discovered they were
plants called "gourds"
and was happy and excited.
He would change them into works of
art and we were all delighted.

Mr. Cleiman made many beautiful things
from all his lovely gourds,
he made baskets, birds, birdhouses and
bowls much too beautiful for words.

He picked the gourds and dried them
and embellished them with twine, he
wanted us to enjoy them,
after all, his work was fine.

Mr. Cleiman brought joy and beauty into people's daily lives that's why his children cherish him as well as his loving wife.

Mr. Cleiman has inspired me to carry on his tradition. He said to follow my hopes and dreams and also my ambitions.

So, I created Gourd Ridge Critters which are funny and heartwarming, there are dozens of them to love and they are undeniably charming.

Hildegourd and Beauregourd are the
oldest of the clan,
Hidegourd's the woman,
Beauregourd's the man.

There are many Gourd Ridge Critters
which you will find unique.
Some are brown, some are green,
and some are even pink!

Hildegourd   *Beauregourd*

So here's an introduction
to my Gourd Ridge Critter friends,
I know you'll fall in love with them
before this story ends.

Gordon

Ramsy

Smiggles

Bert

Hootie

Ivernon

Rastus

Haywood

Oscar

Each time I see a gourd outside
dangling from a vine,
it reminds me of my father
each and every time
I know that he's in heaven with the
good Lord by his side,
but as you can plainly see my friends,
my father hasn't died.
He lives on through my creations and
stays forever in my heart for he
taught me about Life and Love and
also about art.

That is why I wrote this book, and
I know he would be glad,
I wrote this book in memory
of my wonderful, talented, dad,
Mr. Cleiman.

My own gourdian angel.

Author Bio:

Donelle Gress is a unique individual with a passion for artistic expression, humor and has always marched to the beat of a different drummer.

After enduring a difficult and painful childhood at elementary school, the subject of ridicule and bullying, she was still a curious and adventurous child who explored life in the woods and created works of art from found objects. She always strived to be the best at something to make up for her dismal early years. This led her down many career paths at which she always excelled and won awards for her ingenuity yet none of which left her feeling fulfilled and happy. Her never ending quest for happiness was relentless.

In her mid-twenties, she married and was blessed with two lovely and extraordinary children but endured a physically and mentally cruel relationship filled with terror and sickness and finally divorced after five years. She then found herself a single parent of two small children. She remarried seven years later to yet another disappointment and divorced after a shocking discovery about her husband thirteen years later. During this time, she was diagnosed with lupus, a debilitating disease and continues suffering its exhausting symptoms daily. At first it was like living in a nightmare, but these limitations were no hurdle for this dream seeker. Her tenacity eventually pulled her through to face the worst yet to come.

Several years after her last divorce she faced with the death of her father. It was all consuming. Panic and dread ensued. It was too much. It was life altering. It was unexpected. It was the end of her world. Somehow, someway, a force greater than herself placed her in front of the computer, manipulated her fingers and enabled her to express how her wounded heart felt and the gaping hole that was left inside. It opened the flood gates to her soul allowing words and images to splash onto paper like raindrops on pavement.

It is through her life struggles that her dreams, aspirations, and life goals would finally come to fruition. She is now a successful entrepreneur living out her artistic vision in two boutiques of her own. She surrounds herself with women who share her vision and has found joy with her many followers, customers, and people she now calls friends. Her father's passing has inspired this book and has helped her heal and become who she is today, at peace, grateful and joyful.

CPSIA information can be obtained
at www.ICGtesting.com
Printed in the USA
BVHW090742220622
640351BV00002B/16